D0577513

Warm, winter-coat thanks to Sheila and Nan. JG

To Gill, Sarah, Ben and Millie, and in fond memory of Sheila. GC

Text copyright © 2019 by James Gladstone
Illustrations copyright © 2019 by Gary Clement
Published in Canada and the USA in 2019 by Groundwood Books

All rights reserved. No part of this publication may be reproduced, stored in a
retrieval system or transmitted, in any form or by any means, without the prior
written consent of the publisher or a license from The Canadian Copyright
Licensing Agency (Access Copyright). For an Access Copyright license, visit
www.accesscopyright.ca or call toll free to 1-800-893-5777.

Groundwood Books / House of Anansi Press
groundwoodbooks.com

We gratefully acknowledge for their financial support of our publishing
program the Canada Council for the Arts, the Ontario Arts Council and
the Government of Canada.

Canada Council **Conseil des Arts**
for the Arts **du Canada**

ONTARIO ARTS COUNCIL
CONSEIL DES ARTS DE L'ONTARIO
an Ontario government agency
un organisme du gouvernement de l'Ontario

With the participation of the Government of Canada | **Canadä**
Avec la participation du gouvernement du Canada

Library and Archives Canada Cataloguing in Publication
Title: My winter city / James Gladstone ; [illustrated by] Gary Clement.
Names: Gladstone, James, author. | Clement, Gary, illustrator
Identifiers: Canadiana (print) 2018900049X | Canadiana (ebook) 20189000503 |
ISBN 9781773060101 (hardcover) | ISBN 9781773060118 (EPUB) |
ISBN 9781773062761 (Kindle)
Classification: LCC PS8613.L315 M9 2019 | DDC jC813/.6—dc23

The illustrations are in watercolor.
Design by Michael Solomon
Printed and bound in Malaysia

MIX
Paper from
responsible sources
FSC **FSC® C012700**
www.fsc.org

My
Winter
City

James Gladstone

pictures by

Gary Clement

GROUNDWOOD BOOKS
HOUSE OF ANANSI PRESS
TORONTO BERKELEY

WITHDRAWN

My winter city holds early light
around us,
a moment before sunrise,
silent,
still.

It holds warmth a little closer to our skin and our bellies,
and time a little slower, tying laces, pulling mittens ...

trudging, huffing creatures move at the
sluggish speed of snow.

My winter city is a soup of salty slushes, full of sliding buses splashing, spraying, sploshing, soaking walkers on the sidewalk.

Water runs fast down the aisle past wet boots and toboggans,

windows gone all steamy,
riders carried on
their way.

My winter city is a deep-freeze
vision of big icy sled hills
and towers that rise up through
far-away skies,

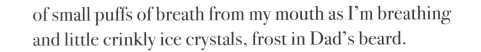

of small puffs of breath from my mouth as I'm breathing
and little crinkly ice crystals, frost in Dad's beard.

The picture is different through the windows of the glass house,
like a warm, rainy summer in a country far away.

My winter city is a wilderness of footprints,
crisscrossing,
disappearing ...

Who walked here before?

An icicle factory, that's my winter city,
all sizes, all pointing straight down to the ground,
where we take our rest on light powder pillows
as heavy thunder plow beasts scrape and clunk.

My winter city is an afternoon journey
past sidewalk singers in shivery shadows,
past winter workers with hot steaming chocolate,
past rows of locked bicycles, buried and waiting,

back where we came from ... backwards sledding.

Jump up,
hang up,
warm up,
done.

My winter city holds us together in a dream before sleeping,

under sheets,
under covers ...

a blanket of snow.

That's *my* winter city.

What's yours?

31901065444194